# Rita
## wants a Robot

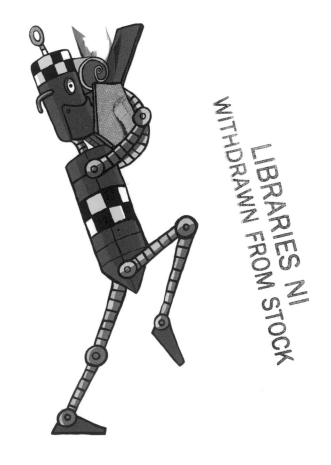

By Máire Zepf

Illustrated by Mr Ando

This is

Rita.

And this is Rita's messy bedroom.

Rita wants
a robot.

A super-sorting robot
that could tidy up the
HUGEST of messes.

Her mum would never tell her off again.

9

And her robot would sort

sort

sort.

Hopefully her robot wouldn't be *too* tidy for her.

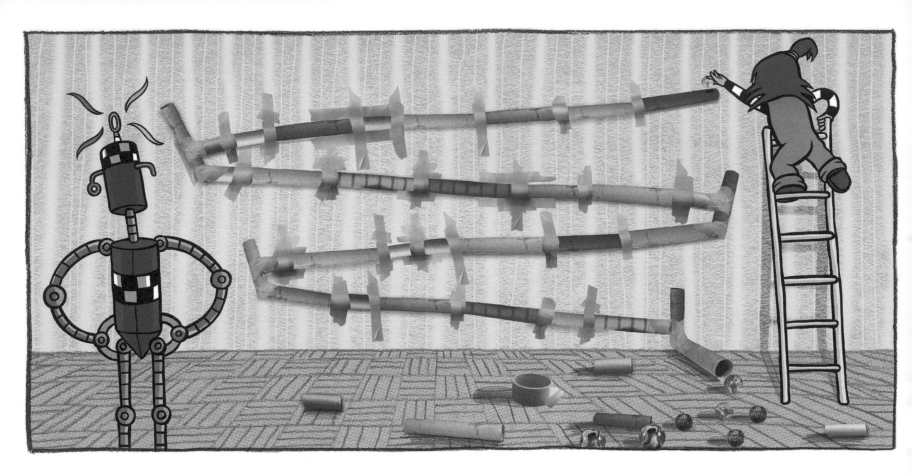

Because that would be no fun at all.

He would need to know when to leave things alone.

Or Rita might get very cross.

What if he tidied things up that are supposed to be wild?

That would be terrible.

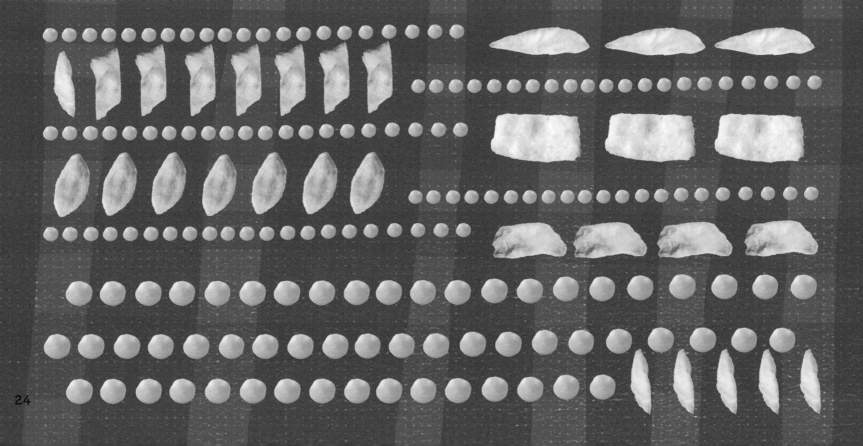

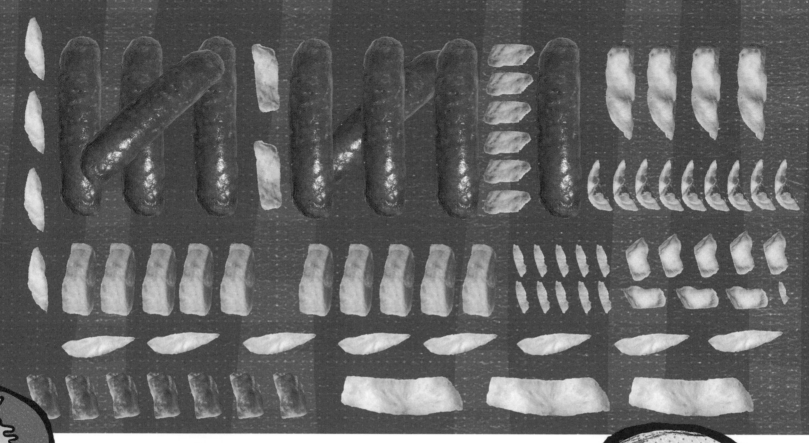

Her robot
could get her
into LOADS of
trouble.

Rita hates
trouble.

This robot could ruin everything.

And where would it end?

29

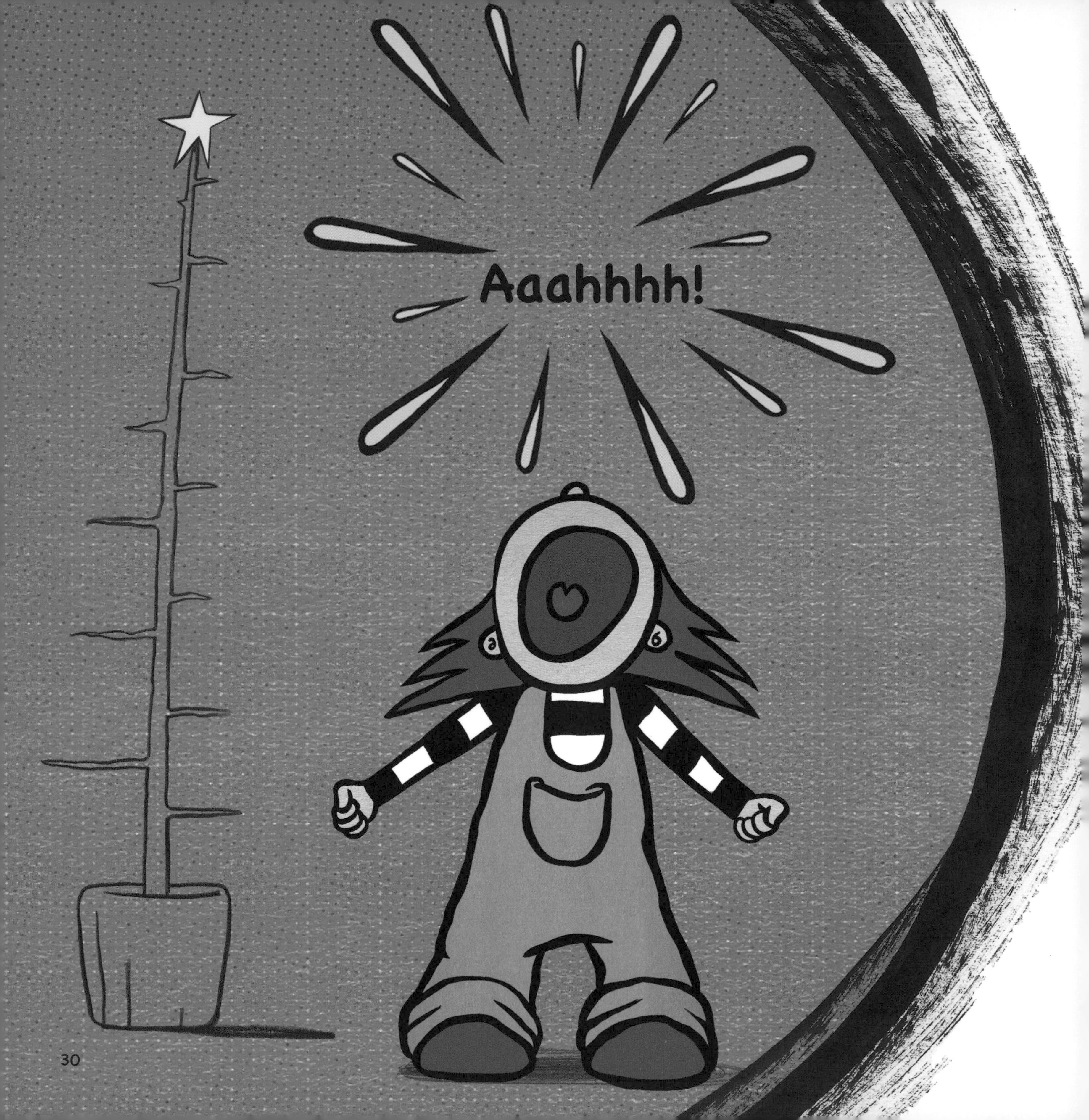
Aaahhhh!

No, Rita has changed her mind.

She doesn't want a super-sorting robot after all.

Rita is better at sorting than any robot.